Tickle Me Time With Stories and Rhymes

By

Sharon Davis

ISBN: 1-4033-7667-0 (E-book)
ISBN: 1-4033-7668-9 (Paperback)
ISBN: 1-4033-7669-7 (Hardcover)

Library of Congress Control Number: 2003090133

This book is printed on acid free paper.

Printed in the United States of America
Bloomington, IN

1stBooks - rev. 02/07/03

TICKLE ME TIME

WITH

STORIES

AND

RHYMES

WRITTEN AND ILLUSTRATED

BY SHARON DAVIS

TICKLE ME TIME

WITH

STORIES

AND

RHYMES

A DELIGHTFUL COLLECTION OF FOUR FUNNY LITTLE STORIES THAT WILL TEACH, INSPIRE AND AMUSE THE YOUNG READER.

Dedication

THIS BOOK IS DEDICATED TO MY LOVING FAMILY WHO HAS SHOWN ME NOTHING BUT LOVE AND SUPPORT IN THE CREATION OF THIS WORK. FOR AMIYA, AMANI AND NEVEYAH, MY PRECIOUS LITTLE GRANDDAUGHTERS AND TO ALL OF MY FRIENDS WHO HAVE ENCOURAGED ME. SPECIAL THANKS TO MRS. JUANITA WALKER, A FELLOW EDUCATOR AND AUTHOR OF "CHURCH FOLK", FOR HER ASSISTANCE AND FRIENDSHIP. I LOVE YOU ALL.

SHARON

BOOK #1

GEORGE GERFUNCLE

IS MY UNCLE

Sharon Davis

GEORGE GERFUNCLE

IS MY UNCLE

WRITTEN AND ILLUSTRATED BY SHARON DAVIS

George Gerfuncle is my uncle and he just loves his A B C's.

Sharon Davis

Uncle Gerfuncle gives an apple to an ant.

He bats a ball with a bumblebee and sees two fuzzy caterpillars in a tree.

Sharon Davis

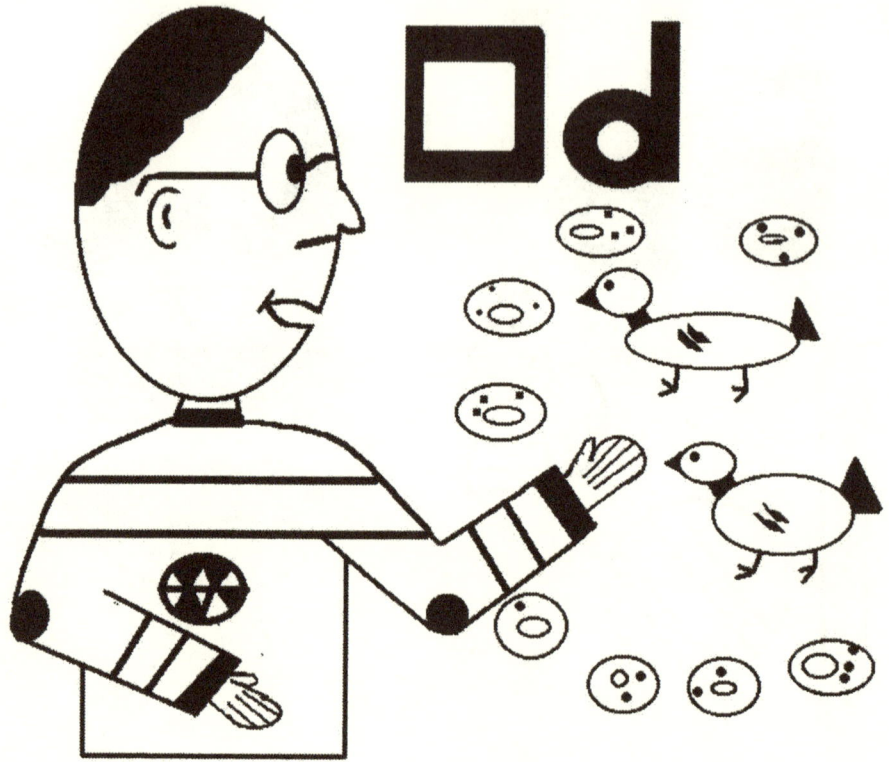

Uncle Gerfuncle feeds doughnuts to ducks.

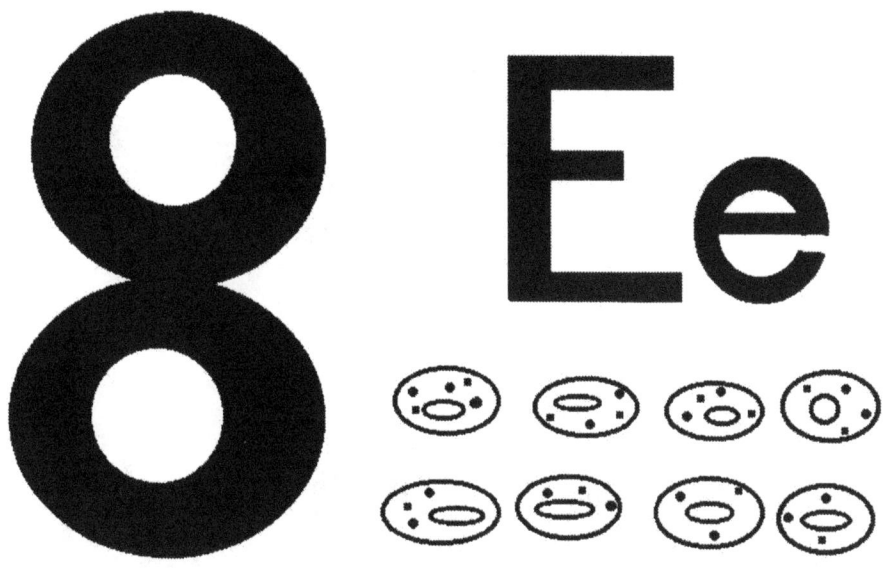

Eight round doughnuts should be enough.

Sharon Davis

Ff Gg

He loves fresh fish, garlic and grapes that are green.

Hh Ii

He enjoys a juicy slice of ham topped with ice-cream.

Sharon Davis

Jelly beans and cherry juice,

Kk   Ll

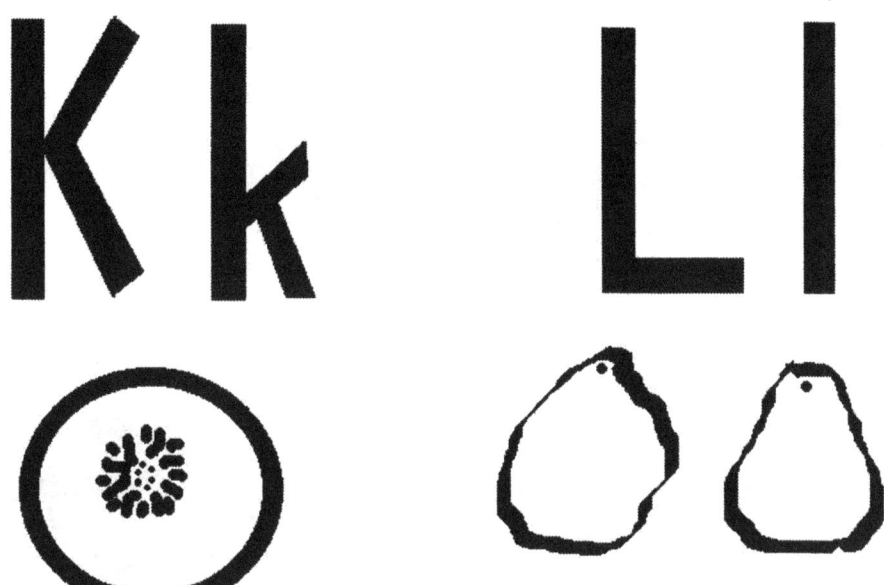

brown kiwi and tart green limes,

Sharon Davis

M m   N n

fresh white milk and crunchy nuts are right on time.

Oranges are juicy and really a treat. Popcorn for snack is great to eat.

Sharon Davis

Qq   Rr

Uncle Gerfuncle is such a quick host. He'll serve you raisins and rice

with steaming hot soup and thick crust Texas Toast.

Sharon Davis

Well, he finally puts up all the food and gets into his van. I think he has something special planned.

He looks at his watch. It is almost time. He is so excited. It opens at nine.

Sharon Davis

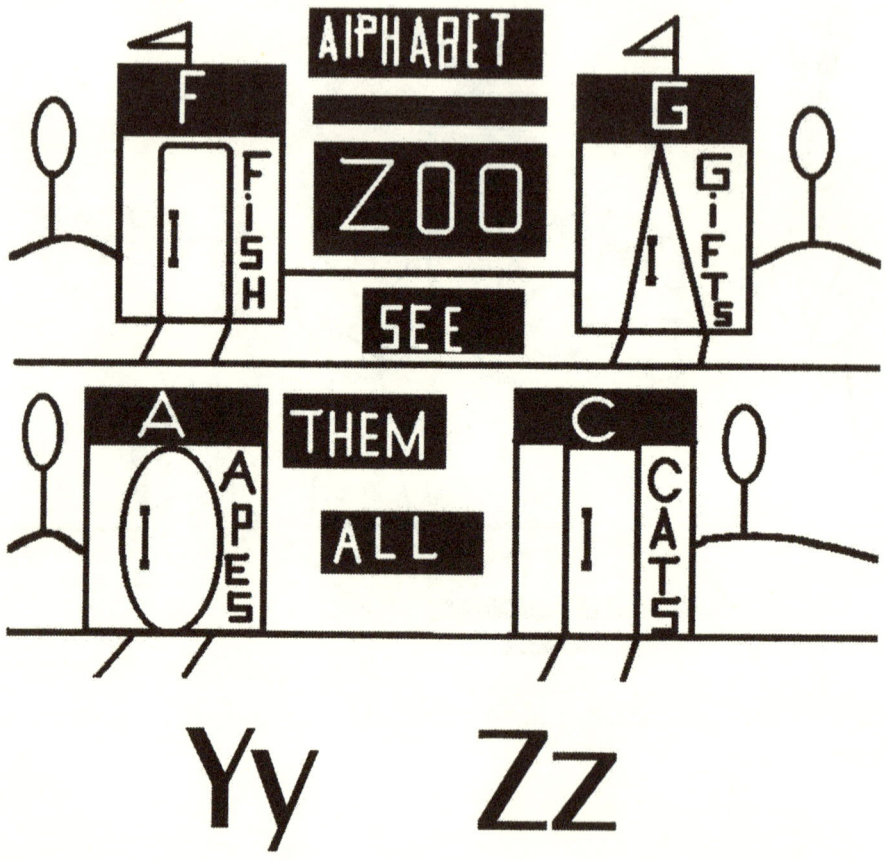

Yy Zz

"Oh! Boy Oh! Boy," he yells for joy. "It's time for the zoo and there's so much to do."

GEORGE GERFUNCLE

IS MY UNCLE
COLOR ME PAGES

AND ACTIVITY SHEETS

Uncle Gerfuncle will visit the zoo. Draw a picture of an animal for each letter of the alphabet.

Sharon Davis

COLOR ME PAGE

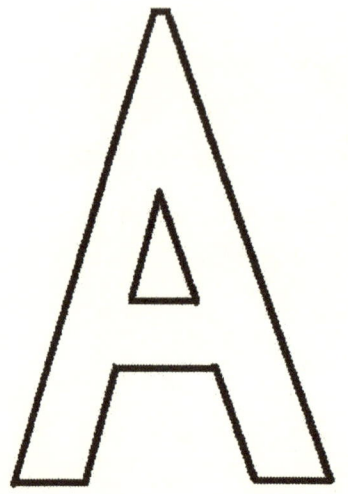

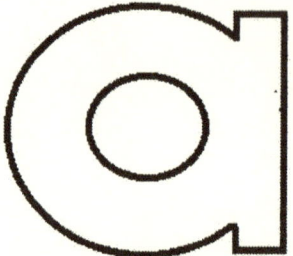

COLOR ME PAGE

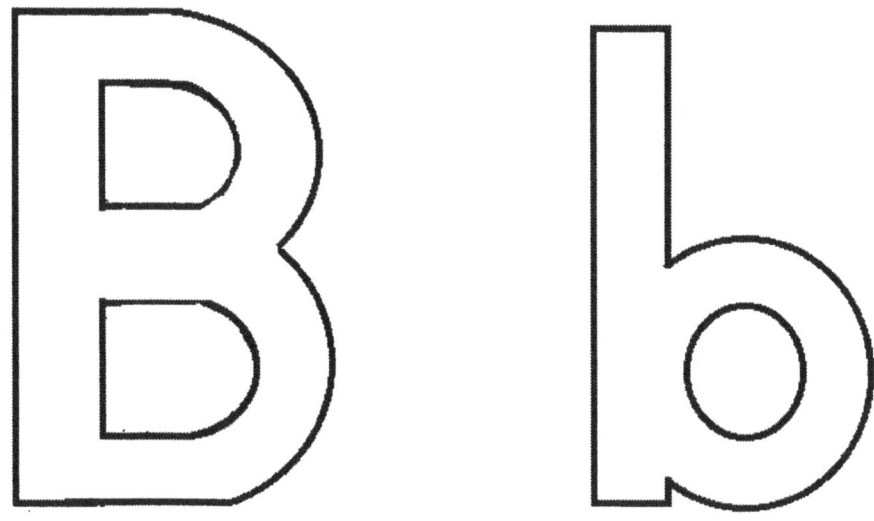

Sharon Davis

COLOR ME PAGE

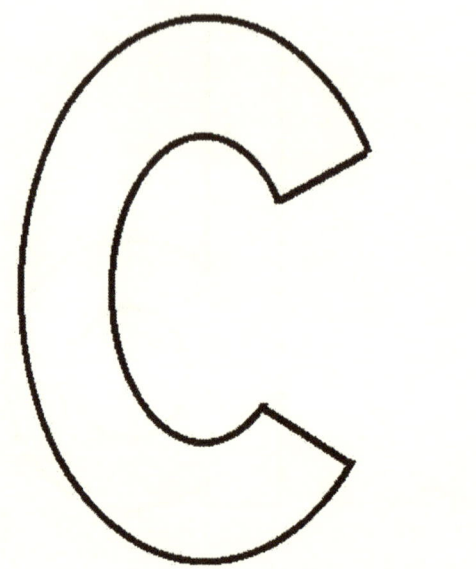
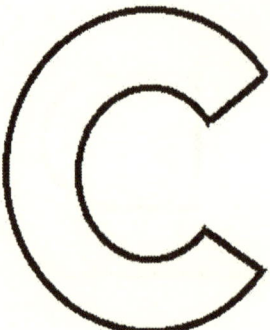

COLOR ME PAGE

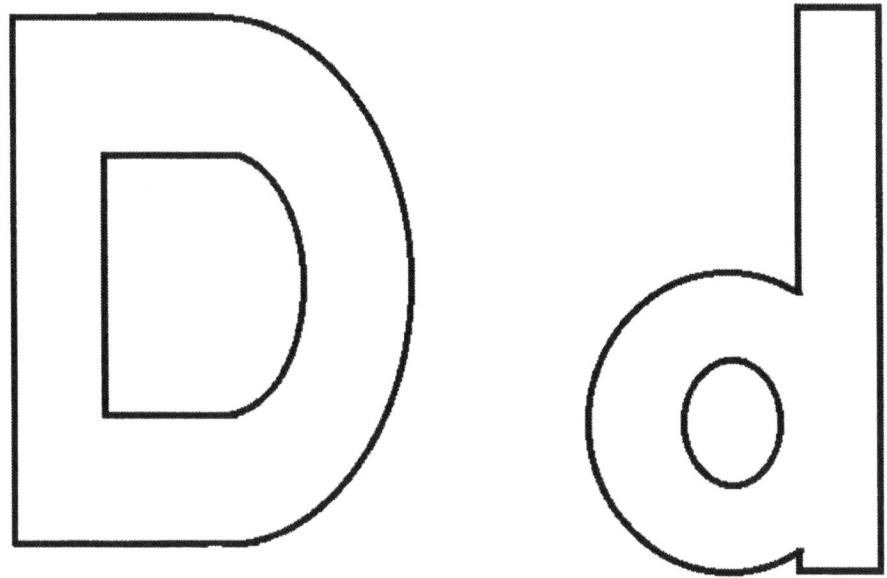

COLOR ME PAGE

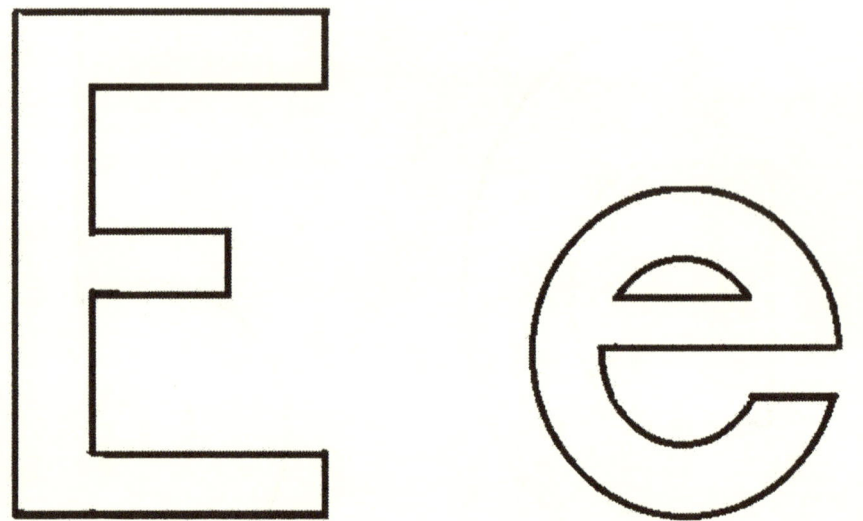

COLOR ME PAGE

Sharon Davis

COLOR ME PAGE

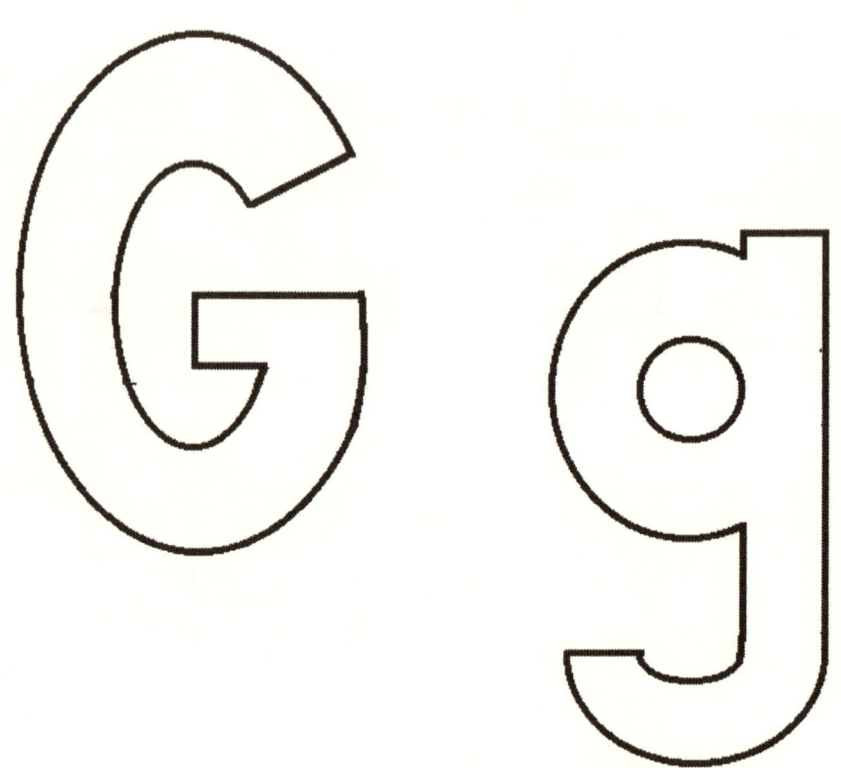

COLOR ME PAGE

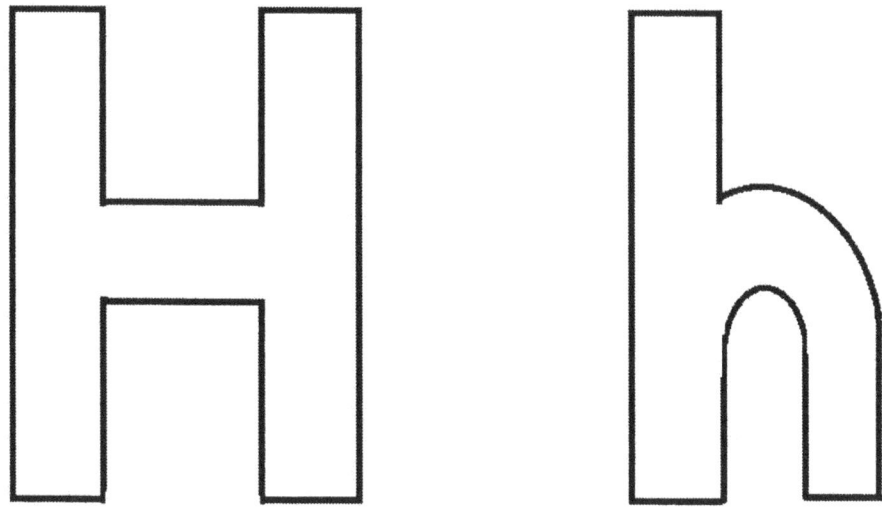

Sharon Davis

COLOR ME PAGE

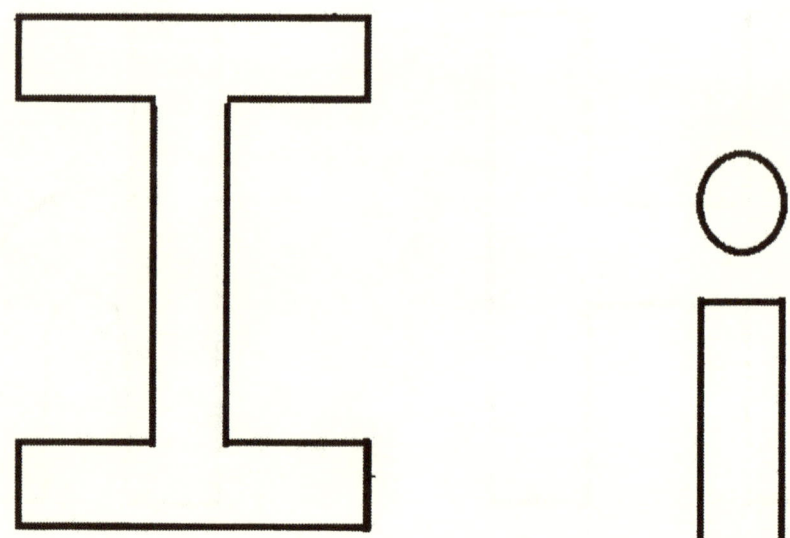

COLOR ME PAGE

Sharon Davis

COLOR ME PAGE

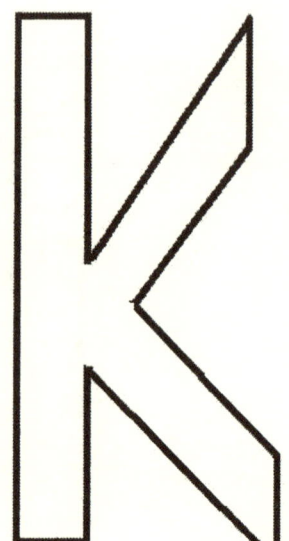 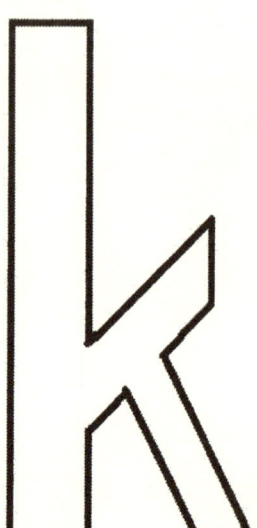

COLOR ME PAGE

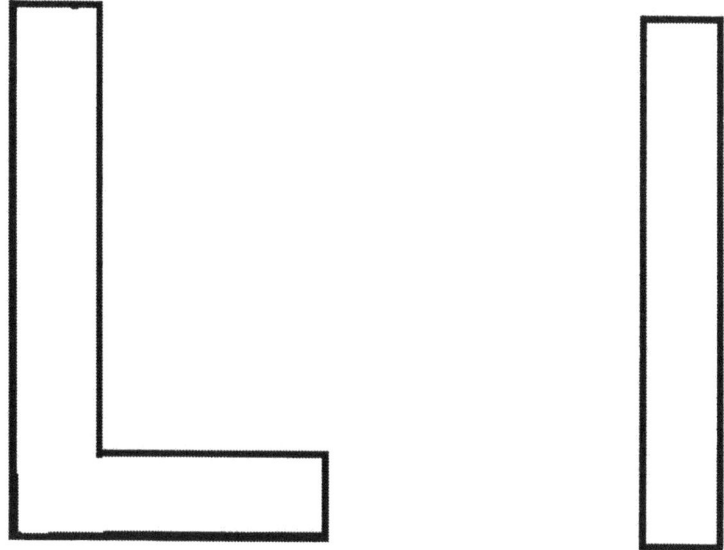

Sharon Davis

COLOR ME PAGE

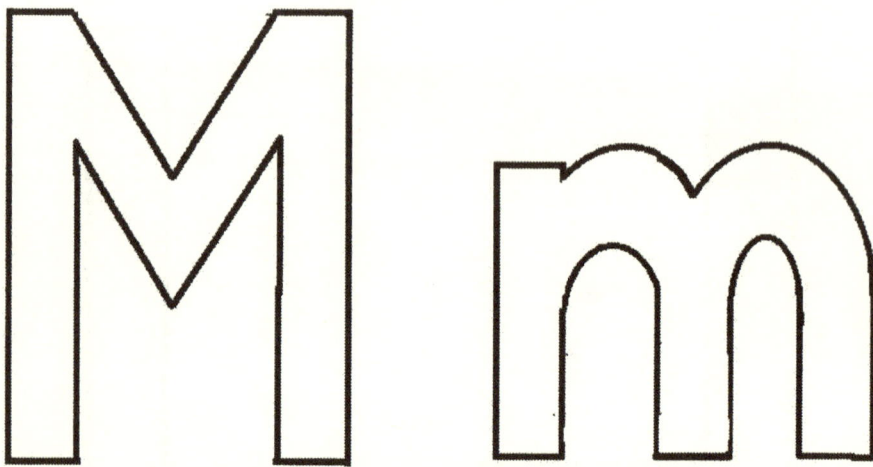

COLOR ME PAGE

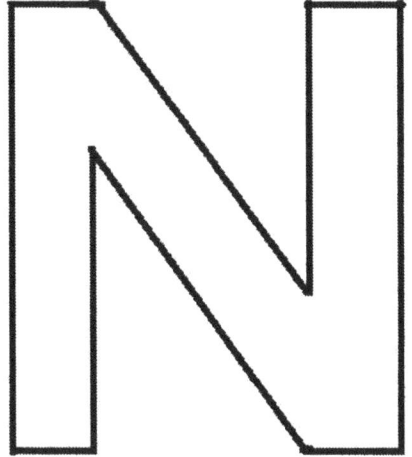

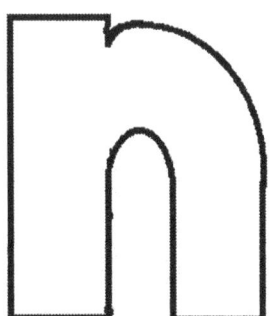

Sharon Davis

COLOR ME PAGE

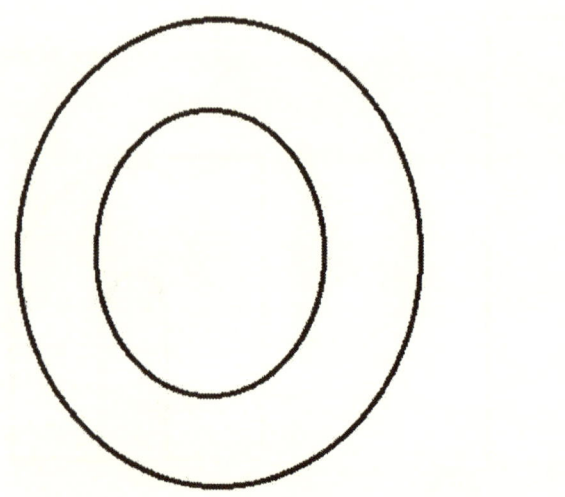

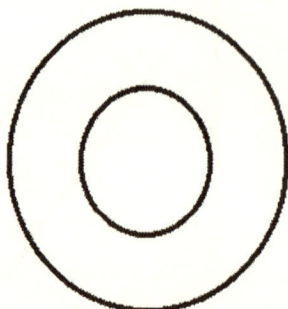

COLOR ME PAGE

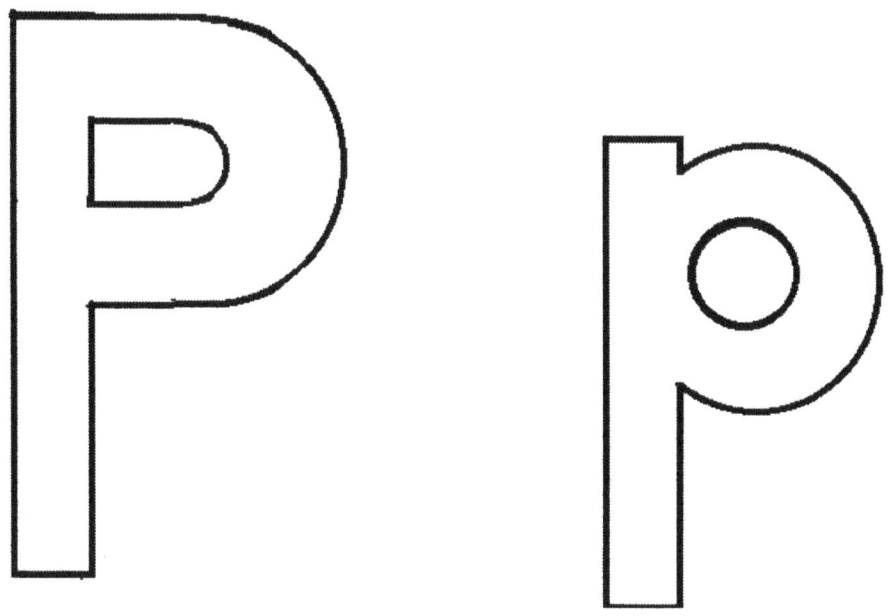

COLOR ME PAGE

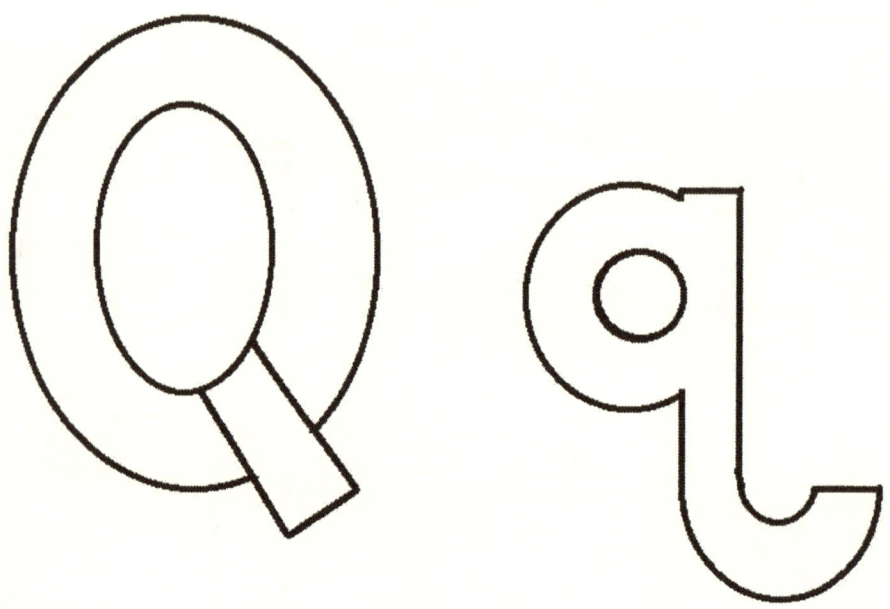

COLOR ME PAGE

Sharon Davis

COLOR ME PAGE

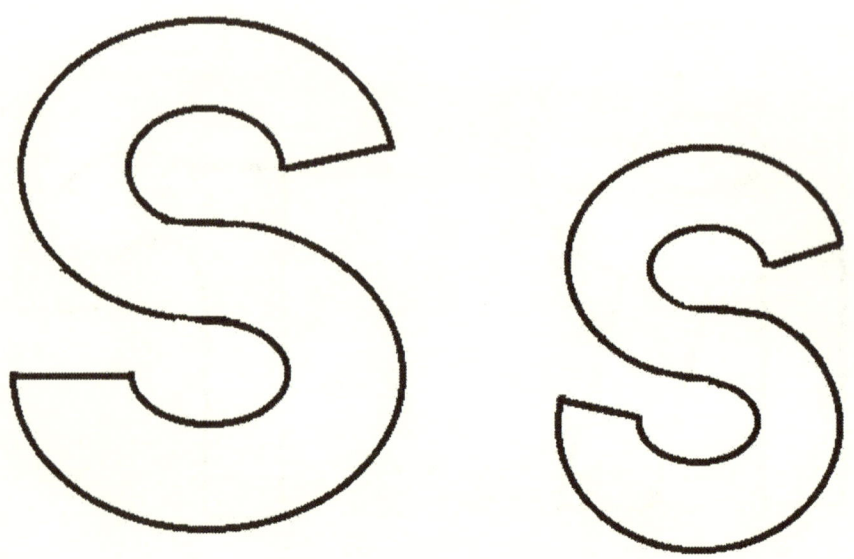

COLOR ME PAGE

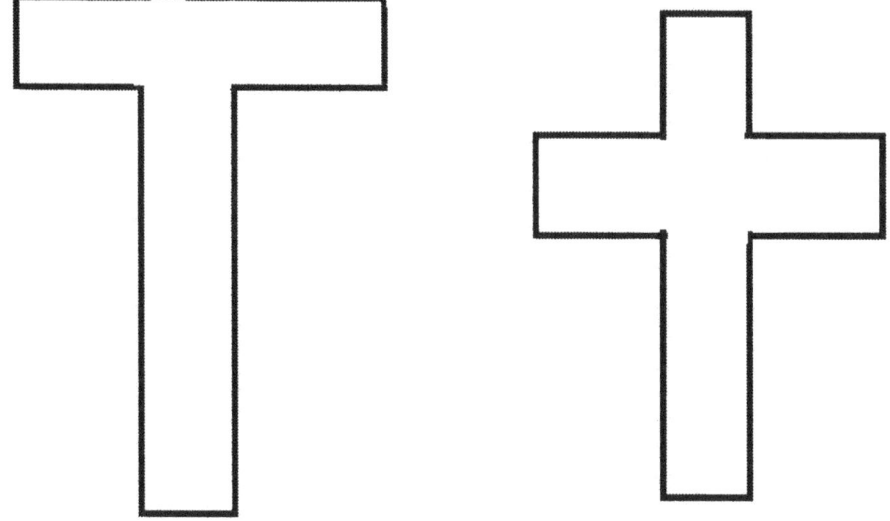

Sharon Davis

COLOR ME PAGE

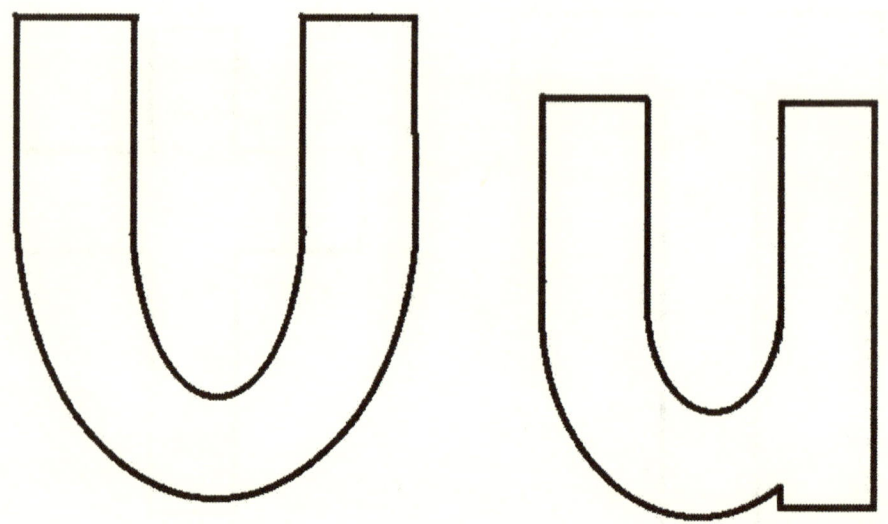

COLOR ME PAGE

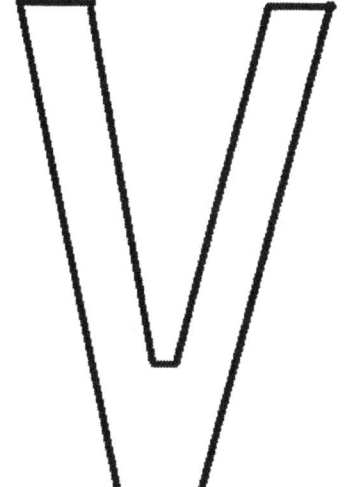

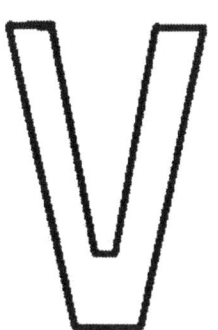

COLOR ME PAGE

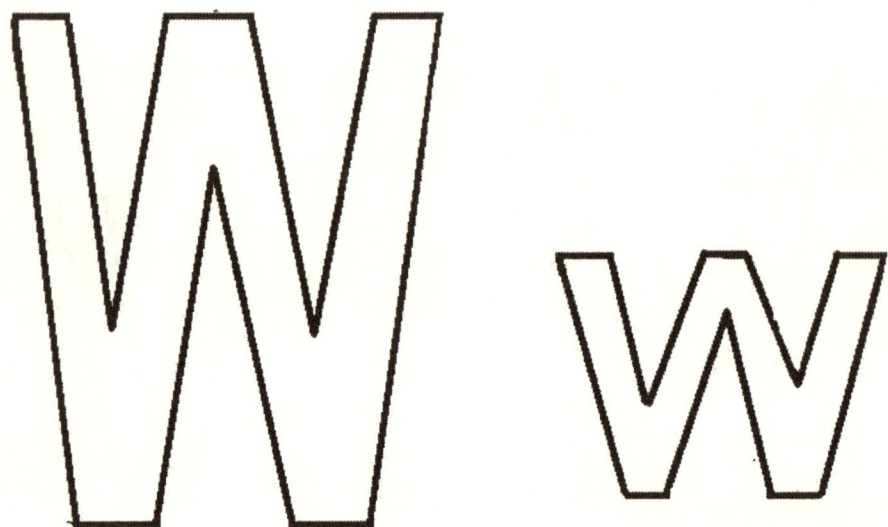

COLOR ME PAGE

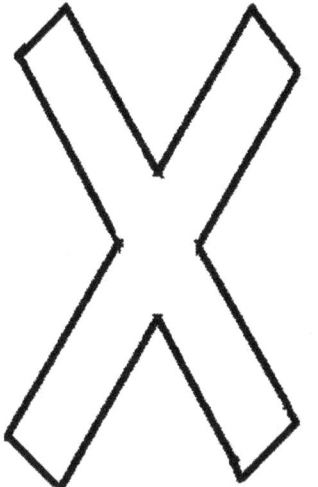

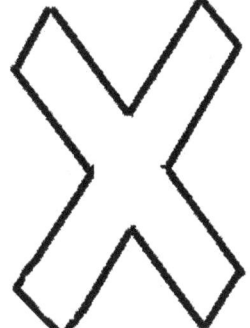

Sharon Davis

COLOR ME PAGE

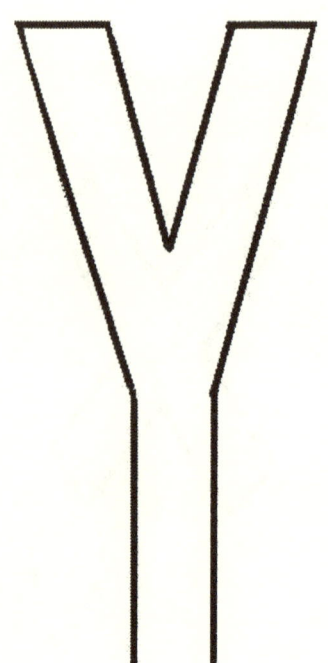

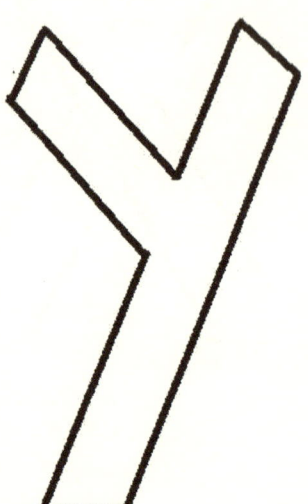

44

COLOR ME PAGE

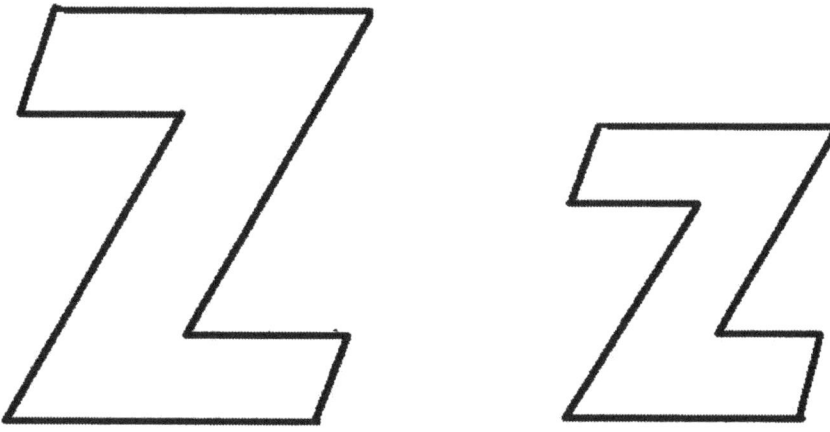

BOOK #2

ANT MATILDA'S

FAVORITE PIE

ANT MATILDA'S

FAVORITE PIE

WRITTEN AND ILLUSTRATED BY SHARON DAVIS

Sharon Davis

It was a beautiful day outside. The sun was shining, the birds were singing and the flowers were smiling.

They were smiling because they could smell the wonderful aroma of delicious pies, cakes, doughnuts and rolls baking in the Cinnamon Shop.

Ant Matilda was already up and about. She was baking all kinds of good snacks and treats for the children who lived on Nutmeg Avenue. This is what she did best.

But today was a special day. Today was the day of the great pie contest. Today was the day that everyone would find out what Ant Matilda's favorite pie was. And oh the prizes! What wonderful prizes to be won. A very large magician's hat complete with a lovely cape and a magic wand. But, the best prize of all is a beautiful picture taken with Ant Matilda and the prize winning pie.

Sharon Davis

Nutmeg Avenue began to come to life. Suddenly, the street filled with the smiling faces of the children who had entered the contest. They had all made scrumptious, delicious pies hoping that theirs would be chosen the winner. They were on their way to the Cinnamon Shop and they could hardly wait.

Amiya, who is six years old, made a pie that she called her Blanket Supreme. That's because some of it ended up in her blanket. A piece is still in there!

Adelyde couldn't decide what she wanted to bake, but finally decided to make a Peanut Butter and Banana Cream Pie. It should be yummy.

George decided that he would make his famous Alphabet Surprise Pie. He knew all of his alphabets, big ones and small ones and their sounds.

Edgar was grinning from ear to ear because he brought his Mashed Potato and Macaroni and Cheese Pie topped with Cottage Cheese. He probably was the only one who would even eat it.

Mahalia Moose even made a pie. A 1, 2, 3, 4 pie. I piecrust, 2 cups of whipped cream, 3 red cherries and 4 licorice sticks. Mahalia loves this pie. It so chewy and fun to eat.

Sharon Davis

The children finally made it to the Cinnamon Shop. As they all entered the shop, Ant Matilda greeted each child with a warm smile and a hug to say hello. She even gave a big moose hug to Mahalia.

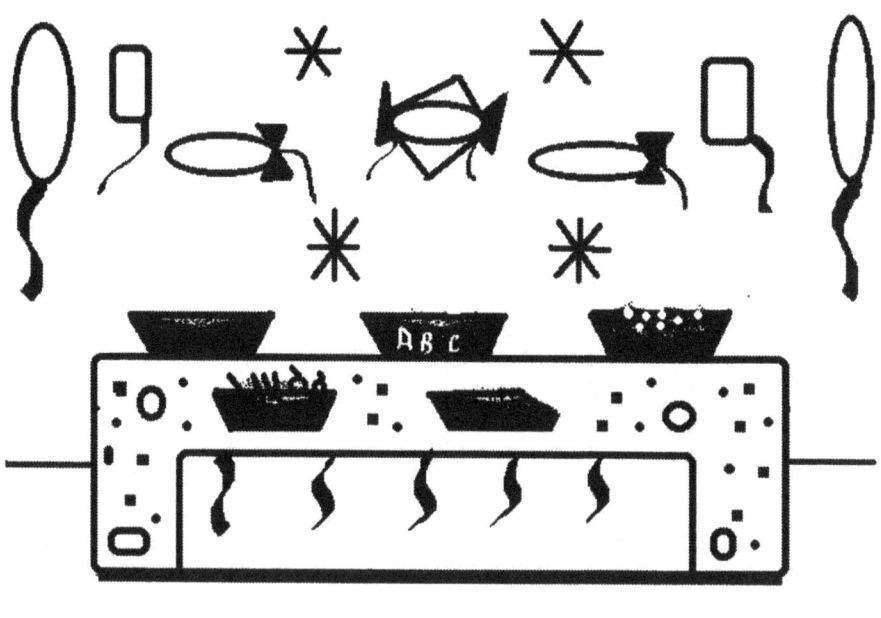

A lovely table was set up for the pies and everyone had a spot. The judging would soon begin. The children and Mahalia placed their pies on the table and waited anxiously for Ant Matilda to start tasting.

Ant Matilda began by saying that she was very glad to see everyone and how delicious each pie looked. She knew that everybody had worked very hard and each pie was a work of art.

She picked up her favorite mixing spoon and started tasting. Amiya's pie was first. "Lovely pie, but there is a piece missing. I wonder what it is? she thought. Then she tasted it. "Hmmm, I taste a little happiness. Very good." She said.

Adelyde's pie was next. "Peanut butter and banana cream, how unique. Oh! Yes, I taste a little joy." Ant Matilda said as she smiled at Adelyde. Adelyde breathed a sigh of relief.

"Well, what do we have here? Why, this is George's Alphabet Surprise Pie." she said. She picked up her spoon and scooped out a nice big piece of pie. "Let me see. Look, here are the letters l o v e. I sure do taste a little love."

Now, for Edgar's pie. "Nice coloring, smooth and creamy and I like cottage cheese, too. Yes, I do taste a little friendship." Ant Matilda said as she winked at Edgar.

Now it was Mahalia's turn. Her's was the last pie to be tasted. Ant Matilda looked closely at Mahalia's pie and said, "It's quite different. I wonder what it tastes like? Wow! I taste a little sharing."

Slowly Ant Matilda walked around the table one more time, smiling and nodding at each pie as she walked. Who was it going to be? She slowly stepped back, looked at each one and said, "Well boys and girls and moose, the winner is…no one! They all looked at each other with sad faces and Amiya almost started crying.

Suddenly, Ant Matilda smiled a big bright smile and said, "My dears, everyone is a winner! My favorite pie is one I can share with my friends. It always brings happiness, joy, love, friendship and sharing to those who eat it. So everyone will get the magic hat, cape and wand plus a beautiful picture of us all with all of the pies.

Sharon Davis

ANT MATILDA'S

FAVORITE PIE

ACTIVITY SHEETS

You want to enter your pie into the contest. What kind of pie would you make? Draw a picture of it and write the name under it.

Sharon Davis

Draw a picture of you, Ant Matilda and all of the friends sharing your pie.

Pretend that you own the Cinnamon Shop. What kind of yummy treats will you have in your window for everyone too see?

BOOK #3

PINK THE BUNNY RABBIT
GOES TO THE HOSPITAL

PINK THE BUNNY RABBIT

GOES TO THE HOSPITAL

WRITTEN AND ILLUSTRATED BY SHARON DAVIS

Sharon Davis

This is Pink the Bunny Rabbit and she has a very big problem. Her little girl, Amiya, has been playing with the loose string in her neck and now she is afraid that her head will come off. She will have to go to the hospital for stuffed animals and she is so scared.

This is Amelia and she is Amiya's big sister. She is eight years old and she has to take poor Pink The Bunny Rabbit to the hospital. Amiya feels real bad about Pink and she needs her big sisters help. Besides, mom told Amelia to do it.

Sharon Davis

This is Amiya. She is Pink's little girl. She is very sorry for pulling the string in Pink's neck and she hopes that Pink will be alright after the operation. She is so glad that her big sister is going with her to the doctor.

Bernard Bear is very worried about Pink. What if the operation does not go well and Pink comes back looking real funny. What will he do? Pink is his best friend out of all the stuffed animals. Well, no matter what, she will always be his best friend no matter how she looks.

Sharon Davis

Kris Cat is also a friend of Pink. She has something special to tell Pink. Kris had to have an operation too. Amiya spilled sticky grape jelly on her one day. They took her to the hospital for stuffed animals and Nurse Needle made a beautiful white velvet patch for her to wear over it. Dr. Sews-A-Lot sewed it on and added two velvet ribbons to make it look like a lovely necklace. Kris wasn't scared at all. "Don't be frightened Pink." she says.

Amelia and Amiya are finally on their way to the hospital. Amiya is feeling kind of scared because she doesn't really know what will happen to Pink. Pink is in the wagon wondering how much longer will it be before they get to the hospital. The hospital is just down the street from their house, so they don't have far to go. "Are we there yet!" she says to herself.

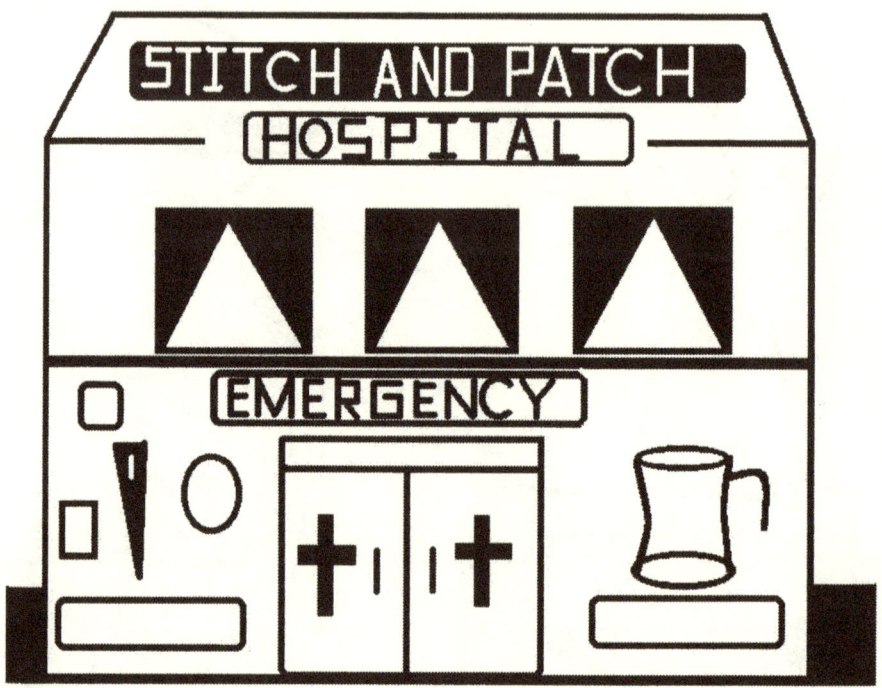

This is the Stitch and Patch Hospital where all stuffed animals and toys come when they need special care. This is where the operation for Pink will be. Doctor Sews-A-Lot and Nurse Needle will take care of everything for Pink. They give the best of care to all toys that are brought in to them. Pink and Amiya have nothing to worry about.

This is Doctor Sews-A-Lot and he is waiting for Pink. "I wonder where she is? I'll bet she is afraid to come in. Why, this won't hurt a bit. Now, where is that Nurse Needle?" Doctor Sews-A-Lot says to himself.

Sharon Davis

Nurse Needle is ready and waiting. All she has to do is get her sewing basket and needles and she is ready to go. "Now where is that Doctor Sews-A-Lot. He's never around when you need him," She says. "I had better go and prepare the table."

Pink The Bunny Rabbit finally made it to the operating room. Nurse Needle made her comfortable and gave her a sleepytime carrot to nibble on. At last, she went to sleep. Nurse Needle prepared the needle and thread and gave it to Doctor Sews-A-Lot. He was ever so careful and stitched and stitched until Pink was as good as new. Now, that wasn't so bad. You couldn't even tell that she had an operation.

Sharon Davis

So the operation was a success. Pink was feeling much better and she was tickled pinker than ever because it was all over and she did not feel or look funny or strange. Amelia and Amiya were very happy. Now it was time to celebrate and have a feeling better party for Pink and her friends.

The three friends had a wonderful operation celebration after Pink got home from the hospital. Kris Cat had delicious cat food, Pink had yummy rabbit food and Bernard Bear had scrumptious golden honey for his snack. After they finished eating, they all had a delightful piece of carrot cake for dessert. Soon, they all began to yawn and stretch. Amiya put them all in bed for a much needed nap. She decided to take one, too. Boy! What a busy day.

BOOK #4

CAN'T DECIDE ADELYLDE

CAN'T DECIDE ADELYDE

WRITTEN AND ILLUSTRATED BY SHARON DAVIS

Sharon Davis

SUMMER IS OVER AND IT'S TIME FOR SCHOOL. TIME FOR
EVERYTHING NEW, EVERYTHING COOL.

MOTHER DREADED GOING SHOPPING TODAY. SHE NEW
EXACTLY WHAT ADELYDE WOULD SAY.

Sharon Davis

SO THEY GOT READY AND GOT IN THE CAR, THE RIDE TO THE MALL WAS NOT VERY FAR.

THEY GOT OUT OF THE CAR AND WALKED UP TO THE
DOOR. ADELYDE COULD NOT WAIT TO GET INTO THAT
STORE.

Sharon Davis

"I WILL NEED LOTS OF TIME TO MAKE UP MY MIND.
EVERYTHING IS SO PRETTY AND NEW. I DON'T KNOW
WHAT TO DO!"

"THE BLUE DRESS IS NICE AND SO IS THE RED. THERE ARE SO MANY COLORS DANCING IN MY HEAD." SHE SAID.

Sharon Davis

"I LOVE THE BLACK SHOES, BUT THE WHITE ONES SAY,
"YES, WE'LL BE LOVELY WITH YOUR PRETTY NEW
DRESS."

"I NEED NEW JEANS AND TOPS TO MATCH AND SCHOOL
SUPPLIES FOR MY NEW BOOKBAG WITH A ZIPPER AND A
LATCH."

Sharon Davis

"THIS ONE AND THAT ONE AND THERE IS ONE, TOO
SO MANY THINGS FOR ME TO CHOOSE."

MOTHER SAID, "HOLD IT, MISS ADELYDE, IF YOU CANNOT CHOOSE, THEN I WILL DECIDE."

Sharon Davis

MOM CHOSE A NICE NEW DRESS AND A BEAUTIFUL
BLOUSE WITH A PICTURE OF A FLOWER AND A LITTLE
CUTE MOUSE.

SHE PICKED TWO PAIR OF NICE JEANS WITH HATS AND
TOPS TO MATCH AND THAT PINK BOOKBAG WITH A
ZIPPER AND A LATCH.

Sharon Davis

SOME SOCKS AND NEW SHOES, HAIR DECORATIONS TOO,
A COMB AND A BRUSH, THESE THINGS SHE CAN USE. FOR
SCHOOL SHE WILL HAVE EVERYTHING NEW.

THEY FINALLY MADE IT THROUGH THE DAY AND HEADED FOR THE DOOR. MOM SIGHED A GREAT BIG SIGH, SHE WAS GLAD TO LEAVE THE STORE. THEN SHE STOPPED AND LOOKED AT ADELYDE, SHE HAD SOMETHING TO SAY. "OH! NO! ADELYDE, CHRISTMAS IS ON THE WAY." BUT THAT'S ANOTHER STORY!!

ABOUT THE BOOK

COME AND MEET UNCLE GERFUNCLE, ANT MATILDA, CAN'T DECIDE ADELYDE AND PINK THE BUNNY RABBIT. THEY INVITE YOU TO COME AND SHARE THEIR STORIES OF LEARNING, SHARING AND CARING. AN INTERACTIVE, FUN BOOK THAT CAN BE COLORED.

ABOUT THE AUTHOR

SHARON DAVIS IS A KINDERGARTEN TEACHER IN GARY, INDIANA. SHE HAS BEEN TEACHING SCHOOL FOR THE PAST TWENTY YEARS AND SHE LOVES IT. SHE LOVES THE INTERACTING AND CONNECTING WITH THE LITTLE ONES. SHE LOVES SEEING THEIR FACES LIGHT UP WHEN THEY HAVE DISCOVERED SOMETHING NEW, WHETHER IT IS LEARNING TO READ OR ADDING TWO PLUS TWO. MRS. DAVIS IS AN AVID READER AND ENJOYS READING TO HER STUDENTS ON A DAILY BASIS. SHE H AS ALWAYS HAD A DESIRE TO WRITE FOR CHILDREN AND HAS USED HER EXPERIENCE AND EXPERTISE TO CREATE FANCIFUL STORIES AND POEMS FOR HER STUDENTS. SHE ENCOURAGES THEM TO USE THEIR IMAGINATION AND CREATIVITY TO CREATE WORK OF THEIR OWN. SHE IS A VERY NURTURING, LOVING AND CARING PERSON AND DEMONSTRATES THIS OPENLY WITH EVERYONE SHE COMES INTO CONTACT WITH. SHE HAS A STRONG FAITH IN GOD AND LIVES BY THE GOLDEN RULE. SHE IS THE MOTHER OF THREE WONDERFUL DAUGHTERS AND THREE ADORABLE GRANDDAUGHTERS.

Printed in the USA
CPSIA information can be obtained
at www.ICGtesting.com
LVHW092153010324
773315LV00003B/589